Civilized Rivers

The bridge walked to and from an adolescence.

Micha Wuulwicce

Written between 1989-1996.

Edited 2019

ISBN: 9781511416931

Hamilton Ontario,

Canada

Dedicated to David Earl.

Thank you for being my teacher and mentor.

Thankyou for the introduction to Rilke, Colette, Benvenuto Cellini...

Thankyou for the innumerable letters that I received from Poland.

Thank you for inspiring my courage to release this collection.

Your heart and mind are beautiful, I am grateful.

Late 1980's, Rosemont Ontario. Photo D'arcy Good

I, *Micha Wuulwicce,* amongst many other things, am a multimedia artist currently residing in Hamilton Ontario, Canada. I have worked as a professional artist, performer, and entertainer in the past, but current circumstances have changed my focus. Life has a beautiful way of presenting all roads that must eventually be taken. For this current momentary purpose, I now, shall be a poet, and a writer of prose.

In the late 1980's I resided in Toronto Ontario, where I trained as a modern dancer and spent a great deal of time sitting, smoking, pondering and journaling. I did this in various coffee shops spread out through the downtown core.

Toronto was a very different city at that time, than it is in 2019. It had a different type of vibrance, it was more affordable and easier to make a living. Although difficult to live as an artist, it seemed that there were always new possibilities, new places to share and perform work around each corner. There was time to sit and ponder, write, smoke (a multitude of affordable cigarettes) and just "be."

I really loved to people watch, and being trained a modern dancer, I was fascinated and interested in the language of the body. It spoke of where people came from, who they were at the present, who they may be in the future. I still feel to this day that actions truly do speak louder than words.

The multitudes of cafes offered many a window seat, and from their *aquarium* view, I would write, draw, imagine for hours. It was a time without cell phones. Cable television was too expensive, so entertainment was found in other places.

Even making plans with friends was not so immediate, telephones did not ring in our pockets, they rang at home, where the message would be recorded, For many of us, we would retrieve the message when we got home, not at work, or on the street waiting for the bus. There was more time, there were fewer emergencies.

So, this is where and when the following body of work is born. A young artist being inspired by his mentors, contemplating and expressing while exploring his spirit through the art of modern dance.

Owls

That decrepit melody ...

scattered my intentions of yellowed Citrine.

The reign of rains,

absorbed the plight of my shallowed desires.

A pure essence within

could no longer be found.

Lay my hands,

nor my heart

upon their healthy lines.

I spent

the multiple numbers of twelve,

sides by sides

by side.

My face is always flattened upon paper.

The wind, with it's violent physicality,

the owls,

all of the faces, all of my souls,

they all lingered.

Each solitaire,

on the one,

horizontal thread.

Each century passing,

with such regret.

Nothing is allowed permanence,

upon geocentric threads,

nor on death's,

sweet

sweet

salty

lips

Unreplenished

I have felt the darkness

within the green lands.

I sunder it

thoughtfully.

I feel quietly

stretched and distorted.

My face searches for the cause,

I feel

the sting of sharpened bicycle spokes,

released, from young angry hands.

A social experiment complete.

Blue tinted screens did not

make the sky bluer.

Nor did green,

add vitality

8

to my withered masts.

Yellow rusted receptacles, ramshackle pencil cutters,

the antique love seats, fastidious patterns.

My oversized nostrils, drawn out with broken crayons.

These are my tangible accomplishments.

My dental flossed,

bubble gummed,

pink carnation

creations.

"I am Sparkling"

during ordinary business.

But now,I have released the sacrificial mouse for the cause.

It's duration is now to be spent inebriated.

My dear sweet sultry serpentine

to be spent on an illusion.

All ment,

to be a mere

unassisted

oral

internal

suicide.

Jack

I do not feel.

I do not wish,

to scrape frost

from the window panes.

Leave it to burn,

leave it to be bitten,

by the sun's persistent rays.

Blessed Be

Blessed be ... for you have mourned.

Yet did we not hold firm?

that morning,

when I possessed the courage

to remain

within those arms?

I vomited

overflowing cups

of childhood memories.

You gained my allowance.

You felt the sight of me,

within the sunset light

of failure.

That sunrise ...

descended,

and burnt fear in the brain.

That sunrise,

bestowed us a power of knowledge,

then the certainty,

of desire.

Then,

you mistook my thirsty words

for the grayest

of our rainy winds.

You became a voice

just walking away.

The shadows of a fruitless fatigue.

Islands

You have always meant more to me,

than just a head, attached to a pair of creative hands.

You and I have always felt like islands,

secluded and all too small.

Nonetheless ...

An island is merely the tip of a mountain,

submerged and hidden,

too scared to allow breathing.

If we choose to exist as islands,

we will be named as islands,

only being known for singular thoughts.

We will be protected

by our fear to explore.

By being unaware,

of our bodies in total,

and by the fabrics we wear,

to ornament and hide.

Take a step and linger.

The island shall rise.

with vulnerability of height.

A very human possibility.

Pockets of Silence

1.)

With what

has my blood

been severely diluted?

Who remains

but the numberless, vacant landscapes?

The shadowless,

shallowness of my mind.

Pockets,

when questioned,

deny the need to be filled,

or to be impregnated.

They lack an archetypal symbol,

(they own syllables expressed freely,

by their own illegitimate mouths).

The illegitimate legitimize the illegitimate.

Do not value the man who owns a severed tongue.

One that remains pocketed and silent.

One that never maintains the truth

of an opinion.

The dog, the parrot,

agreeing to all disciplines received.

Beware empty pockets and spirits.

2.)

I, have accompanied a different guide.

A flowered head of pink abundance,

curving it's fertile skull,

offering me a ride.

Purple thistles contained in acrylic eggs.

Yellow, yellowing and turning brown.

All resembling my spirit,

crying out

some other

Father's name.

It has echoed,

exited

and existed

concrete amongst my thistles.

Whispers and whispers and whispers,

becoming as deadly,

and as sun dried,

as my casual heart.

3.) Emptied Pocket

Your love for me was sudden,

yet

an earthquake away.

My sorrow would be caused,

from waiting for you

in our bed.

Your next heartbeat.

Your next heartbeat.

Your next heartbeat.

pause

I asked...

"May I sleep in our bed?"

Silence ...

Produced was a bed of nails.

4.) Lost Pocket

You carry the ability to tear and puncture

but you have left me with only a bruise,

there,

on the left side

of my purple dying heart.

No medal or trophy had been taken,

you are indeed the medieval soldier.

Your eyes tell of the tale,

your purpose lost,

your will to survive dead.

Un-dispatched love letters - number one

Dearest Robin,

dearest bird of flight.

Temperamental winds have swallowed my wings,

reduced my speed of travel,

reduced my life.

Let us meet at the edge of two sources,

behind the earth's shadow,

between the waters,

to find the congregations of resources.

The remains left on sandy shores,

debris caused and crushed.

Two resistances,

find the subtleness of distance,

within their harmony.

There upon the sands

are the skeletons,

no longer named or known.

Fatigue is the cocoon

that had melted upon their tongues.

Distance is the shelter created,

that no longer holds a benefit.

Love is a triangle's weight.

It's disintegration

is my key,

that will open to a clearer sky.

Angel

Distance yourself, from that which is feared,

There is a weight, there is gravity.

Ceiling plaster patterns have fallen much closer,

but the deep lying mis-truths

refuse to move.

There is no sense of earth under the calloused foot.

Toes are reaching for the touch of splintered wood,

 and the cold, rusty nails.

I wish to hook the bursting vessels.

The grounding wire has been sharpened for injury.

Brown and bruised, screaming hoarsely,

a genius calls out for recognition.

He confers for a meeting with the divine,

his work is complete.

He requires directions to new equations and dilemmas,

or at least

partial answers.

Perhaps even the romance of

disdainful consequences.

No God arrives ...

on the 3:41 train.

The train was much too slow,

for those who have the impulse,

to follow the road leading to salvation.

Who was it?

That had been saved during the christening?

The ghost of possibility?

No ...

not I the ghost,

... no.

Yet there was an angel,

too spectacular to be recognized by name,.

It arrived to enumerate all of the marked souls,

for planned future captivations.

Look!

Squint ...

Listen!

Look!

Squint...

Listen!

Look!

Squint...

Listen!

No God comes

as of yet,

on the 3:41 train.

Meanwhile ...

every

body

passions,

to repeat

all the better known

sins.

Cessation

This is not a time for eggs to be found,

or robin blue eggs to be laid.

Warmth is sent

or spent through incubation,

a provided warmth from the skin.

Not from stones

tossed through indifference.

Stones burnt and fuelled,

and then cooled,

quick-silver dry.

This tender kiss could not be left as last,

those large lips, I met in darkness,

pious visits, I made into that bed.

Sweat.

The odour of two paints melting,

eyes glint from different nights,

breathing in unison.

A choice, of permanence.

No promises lie.

Ideals hang on rusty nailed hope.

No guarantee of incoming tides,

or pass of seasoned cycles,

or warming of hearts yoked.

It never seemed to be *natural* ...they said.

Forget Me Knots

Blood upon rustic razor blades,

only once used.

They are discarded,

within empty fields

where

my children no longer play.

For fear of cutting a calloused foot.

They have often fallen victim,

to splinters,

retracted from my spine.

From these ancient hands,

that have shown my age,

long before my mind,

they have indeed

fled.

Sparrows

I have discovered double blades,

driven deep and steadfast,

between two packaged ribs.

I have searched.

to find a strengthened,

sinuous hand,

to pull them out

of my emotional destitution.

Drying lips,

like that of hardened leather.

Fingertips,

press against the peel of skin.

A small thought ...

A soul must journey,

for fear of the death,

for fear of the failure,

in any attempt of the ritual,

we have named

merely as survival.

There is a fear of silencing a heart,

that beats out in desperation:

The sorrow,

of possessing the intuition,

which is merely,

the human capability of becoming an empathetic.

Roads

I have found the configuration

of the alternating winds,

the ones that blow

inaudible translations.

I am waiting for the messages,

as the air grows thin.

I have created pathways

to those less cherished.

Those,

who live on the roads

long,

long since filled.

Within my mouth I carry a package,

produced by porcupine quills.

I communicate through ether,

I throw silver balls of stone.

Listen!

Rhythmic feet are still beating,

upon a distant,

burnt,

root filled

floor.

On this ground,

men exhaust themselves breathing,

pursuing love, pursuing war.

The earth is like a pool of blood,

contemptuously bleeding.

It is stiffened by two souls breeding,

condemning those that love in trust.

I have carried weapons with no meaning,

to murder

my leering unknown,

I felt my heart stop beating.

I see

that your soul

has flown.

Arianrhod

The reverend's bullet did assist,

in rendering a footman's journey,

to that of a mere circle.

No empathetic smile could endure,

a steadiness of lip and tongue,

self-denial,

and false pride.

The statuesque Virgin Mary...

dropped the stone from within.

Fatally,

24

she did admit ...

That a virgin could exist,

only at one time:

When a person could walk

across the tooth,

of their God,

and not be consumed

by the very breath,

of the one deemed

as their creator.

Gananoque

Rock lichen green,

peat moss shelves of aching

raking red brick.

Whitened, white fungus felt.

Reddish root, Scottish pine,

(spider webs, covers, crawls),

cracks the granite,

flicks of the sparkles white.

Cutting the rocks

Mother Nature's tongue.

Evening comes.

The current moves me.

This rock,

hearty

and whorish whole,

has felt a temple,

of a religious grace.

Into the stony shards of puzzles:

Frozen green apples

of rippled waves.

Broken thumbs and doubled wrists,

26

the green tinge

of the eyeball tidal lids.

Peat moss shelves.

White are bones

that cry into dusk,

as they tell

of a timely dust.

They are begging for a memory

to be

borrowed.

Undispatched Love Letters – no. 2

Dearest David,

I have never considered you to be some saint of God.

Your endeavours never did pertain to the

I.

Your angelic fortifications caused decay.

I had been your soul,

and then was left

without a carcass.

Half an empty face,

a vase with only broken stems,

and my hands,

sand could cut, as if they were splinters.

Elbows, forearms, knees and shins,

all the bruises,

all the hairline cracks.

... He did not notice the blood left on his collar,

but later,

I would find his shirt discarded.

I Always Feel.

I Always Feel.

I always feel ...

I lay in the bed holding Jeannette's book close,

I awoke, startled, with no torn pages.

What if you were to find a body?

I found the blood spattered upon the doorstep,

I found locks of hair discarded in hallways,

I found the empty easel ... wet.

I found the last brush stroke falling off the canvas.

I have found your cigarette burning,

all the daisies plucked

on the floor.

I searched for the warmth of your fingerprint in the nowhere.

Doesn't death wait and mock

every daydreamer?

Photo Booth Portraits

Life bestowed amongst healthy limbs.

The essence of youth portrayed,

upon faces not yet marked,

by scorn, malice,

sorrow, pity, deceit,

or the satisfaction,

of being wise.

We possess a blissful ignorance,

that age does act as the grand deterrent.

That, there is a limitation,

referred to as time.

We are vandals,

before white walls.

determined to leave a mark.

We refuse to leave useless words,

so we leave

you.

At seventeen

I catch,

the life.

I send my regards to the wind,

but cannot catch it's scent.

I can feel a warm tongue,

lick and taunt my ears.

I find myself ...

unable to taste it.

I cannot feel the warmth,

of my own presence.

Perhaps it is the wind?

Speak from a heart,

like it does not know it's own soul

... it said.

Then, later,

I found the fingerprints,

of the ones who had touched me.

I am allowed to measure scars,

self inflicted,

by some other,

wise method of injury.

Who was the first?

Who is that proverbial *lamb*?

The one

that you never identified as

your slaughterer?

Arboreal fabrication

It climbed with resistance,

a sudden drop from seclusion.

The leafless skeletal stave,

had stretched desperately,

to hush it's evident upheaval.

Spiralling inward forms.

Coniferous and sloping in descent,

they had created a state unlike existence,

a baptismal plunge into lapidation.

The sanctuary of no longitudes,

implantations or suspensions

Placed upon deciduous ground,

it masqueraded

as a child beaten breathless in the shadows.

As a faux maiden who wilfully consented,

to remove the facial shadows,

created by "her" own hair.

The accusers ...

condemn.

Determine ...

the peculiar sight of saplings.

Anticipate ...

all foreseeable injuries.

Balance and dissect.

If lips it did possess, it would secretly surrender

all possibility of resolution.

Thus withholding all of its rich secrets,

from those who do not value possessions.

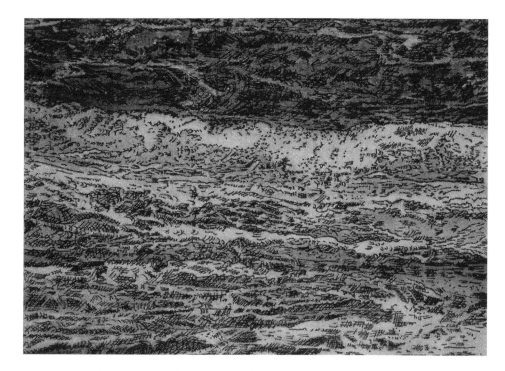

Conversation on Decay

Speak

of men who are dead.

Never known,

or seen on an extended hand.

The faces that no longer reach

or animate

any individual expression.

Once there had been a splendid aura lying,

within my trembling hands.

Now

I cannot fertilize

this discarded cloak.

Death is a silent shadow,

leaving no temperature after its caress.

It leaves a permanent silent script.

Alcoholic

How

do I detest,

the sound,

of ice cubes,

neutral and pliable as plexi,

falling into his glass,

Erase it,

rub it down,

rub it out,

the chalk and the slivers.

All into the floor to be buried,

with the scents of dead cabbage,

and the mutated

cat-pawed mice.

One,

cannot erase a sound,

only wait,

for its dissipation.

Those lips,

hiding grey, false gums,

stretched over ivory teeth,

alloy alcohol searing, cigarette tips.

Nostrils flair only to suck a mere breath,

are thus stained a permanent yellow.

Rosiness of cheek,

can only be achieved,

through

one

more

drink.

No natural endeavour could achieve,
the same healthy smile.
Embalming is a procedure,
not meant for the living.

Number sixty four

LoM 1Ao

In this house
no eagles have flown,
they lie dusty and brittle,
balancing on their beaks.

I climb the stairs,
marvelling at the loss of wings.
I search for a room where I may allow a breath
upon an ancient mirror.

Here
... there is a haunting.

The fact remains,
that the father has died,

eyes are his and empty round,

readily willing to fall from sockets.

Is this the body,

where his life was lived?

These eyes lit his face,

now pale lined.

Yes ...

I could chase the last love

remains,

from my heart.

The words have always been the same,

captured and contained.

He would search the floor,

the tongue moved like a spoke revolving.

In the end no arrows flew,

his soul now

ground dusty blue.

Where is that man?

Who whispered solitudes,

and erased my footprints?

Stranger Dispositions

have only occurred,

when shadows consume the weaker realms.

A human behaviour.

Only a carcass would assume,

that every intent of movement,

is initially still,

by that

of a quiet fetus.

Honeycomb, catacomb,

octagonal diagonal.

The hand is a multitude of triangles,

with evident smoothness,

but nonetheless sharp,

when inspected under the lens.

This square microscopic eye,

allows no distortion of force,

nor allows no full faced telegram

with impeccable DNA.

Health is only a vision,

perceived with meticulous eyes.

Those who seek the surface beauty

realize ...

That true health is a constant achievement,

not a goal to be attained.

Legends are better to be pursued,

to be possessed,

by a youthful empty mind,

for they have no recorded history,

to base their miscalculations.

The aged are retainers,

their memory is a beauty,

it is a memory which maintains their history.

David

I flew my kite,

but it was tangled

within a dream.

Damn! Dusty meteor trail!

Stroked the darkest of cat eye nights,

I flew my kite under broom lit light,

sweeping the bowels of the air.

David, I say,

I whisper David...

David...sleeping?

38

Dreaming

...weeping.

My soul has fallen,

has been felled.

Spiral down, down

upon the pavement of a charcoal brood.

A dirty, dark smudge of life.

I have tried to come prepared.

I flew my kite,

in search of my soul.

It wishes to prosper within its own solutions.

Produce its own illustrations,

and reject that octagonal squall,

that cries out and screams,

a diligent and distant rhythm.

It rejects my resolutions.

Rattle, rattle,

my heart is failing, flawing.

A considerate choice for a prevailing wind.

A considerate choice for a distant hum,

of a knot being tied,

of a snake rattle riddling.

I flew my kite into a heaven with no meaning,

The man flies high,

with tools for safe cracking,

and spinal fluids,

drawn from men with reputation.

I flew,

I flow,

I fly...

Then ...

There in this feather felt, hairline crack,

a sliver of a kite's tail appears,

being pulled by a soul that I had once named

as my own.

"HELLO!!!"

I have cried, I have screamed.

Silent ponder ...

tap fingers on Pandora's box.

Then

the soul

fell through a cloudless voice,

spiralled down,

down.

Lingered...

sighed,

slipped within a medieval crack,

and disappeared.

Oh ... !

oh,

oh!

I whispered but did not breathe.

David ...

David, I say...

I whispered, David,

David!

Leaping ... leaping,

dreaming,

weeping ... he awakes.

"My soul has flown, has fell.

David, the world is gone ...

growling, and sour!"

David?

Separation at 48

We shall meet once again,

Carrying silver snails between our toes,

tickling our ribs with driftwood whips,

between two rhythms,

between two souls.

When I fly the kite,

I hope to entangle it,

within our dreams.

Swooping up,

and up,

it turns on me,

strings burn on me.

No dream,

is tangled,

within the spider's row,

across from the fishnet

within the snow.

Yet ...

Your soft brown hair has crawled inside,

call it green.

So ...

so ...

so...

I hand you a brush,

to smooth out the wrinkles,

within your leather fist.

Scotty

Analyze, analyze.

Do we dare copulate,

without a personal conviction?

Reason enough, to do what we are expected.

Bring new lives into the world,

It is suggested,

that with time

you will love them.

Time does pass,

or at least ... it is said.

Hence we die.

Or, so it is said.

Small Spider

To...

no one

have I offered the security

of a twelve foot coven cross.

I only offer the Pagan's dream,

the search for a nomadic destiny.

I offer no satanic nightmare,

nor bristles,

that leave pine needle scars.

So take my bed of pine,

the one,

with the soft

green cones,

to cushion your heavy head.

It has felt the burden of spells,

larger than your own.

This pine is offered

resistance from my tongue.

It has an unfamiliar bite.

No babes have bloomed with injustice here,

in this boat,

in this vessel.

It floats toward the rock,

with dreadful trees scowling.

They pull us under, the overhanging brush.

The rocks stroke and scrape the bottom,

a resting place is earned.

Allowed to stand,

I urinate over

the side of this boat.

Small spider crawls along the thumb,

as the liquid crashes,

against the red root.

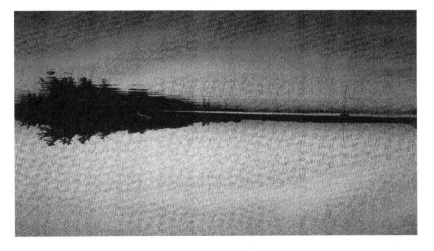

Red Canoe on the St. Lawrence

Alive and growing.

A pungency with depth,

it allows a fermentation,

one which is quite alive.

It takes hold.

of silky strands,

hairlike, root brains,

that devour to suffice and sustain.

I am swept into a body where all wood drifts,

rests with *fishes*,

the snails,

and then clam shells.

A revealing collection

of unmarked shiny greens.

There is forgiveness

lying here,

concerning the cycles of death.

An acknowledgement

of the natural progression.

Unified partnerships and interconnections.

I found an extreme,

in a strange tranquillity,

a hum.

Between the floors,

I was elevated,

by the pinch of uncertainty,

the surprise.

I am left frightened,

by the unrecorded,

unseen numbers

of the faceless.

I hear them murmuring,

being recorded,

by inhuman sources.

I search the shore for red rocks,

of enormous sizes.

I feel a selfish need to carve

my epitaph.

I do not.

The Blue Heron guides me, in a crescent moon,

half an island is mapped.

Dragon flies,

fluorescent aquatic marine.

The lilies green,

fade to white stems,

hang dragging,

like a lazy dog's tail.

I hover,

in my craft.

Sun hovers over me.

Burns, bringing the gift of freckles,

to be joined together later,

by age.

Agatha Schwager

I have found a woman,

who produces the visual doctrine,

a dictation on the aspects of birth.

Her hands have received daughter and son,

and now she renders the act of creation.

Diaries of the unseen blood,

the endearment of birth,

the truth.

Black off grey,

brown into yellow,

the inkling of white semen seeds.

A white canvas is her carcass,

from where she carves the earth,

wet and as dry as skin.

She is a sculptress.

she moulds them intuitively,

the minds of women, children and men.

She has revealed

bluntly,

the remote woman giving birth alone.

A truth,

the whispered fears of cowering cats.

Adam's Rib

A squall causes great use in fortification,

as purposes lie awake,

within and without.

Then...

there is this neon fluorescent fish,

that swam in...

awkwardly.

(under the influence)

Dismissing it's social skills

it demanded a result,

not a theoretical possibility,

not a subjective grant of asylum,

no list of superficial failed endeavour.

Merely a result.

Only a conclusion,

the simple answer.

Bloor in December

From within this cave,

shallow views of a mother,

the one,

that twists inventions.

Pats of neon light.

Twenty-one inch flicker,

the *faming*, gleaming,

football tumblers.

Watching.

Christmas trees,

cut and dried,

hung suspending.

Yellows,

of plastic braiding ropes,

wild oranges.

Extensive chords,

No snowing fall,

to cover all,

thick-aling,

trickling,

bay-sky,

bird sky.

Starling

with the lung of moon.

Ye ole Brunswick houses,

one thousand, eight hundred, seventy six.

Provides no mandatory recall,

upon the tackled sign...if...I.

It do hurt,

like the sun's thoughts,

hip...no tides,

slowly.

Whiley winds,

no ledge of delay.

Waiting, wondering for toad's hop,

hopping to disentangle,

wistful...fly.

Responsibility

Gentle lambs,

bring all winter snows,

with much reverence,

but little desire,

to influence new growth.

A scent is brought,

with the fire of the season.

It is accompanied with a memory,

of that which is aged.

It is as influential,

as bones growing.

I wish that I was able,

to meticulously sweep,

away my bare footprint.

I wish

that I could lose the responsibility,

of leaving

the guiding path,

soon to be followed,

by another.

Jessica

Walk down to the lake with me,

perhaps there,

we will be granted

words.

The Gods shall grant us the gift of a poem,

if we choose to dwell,

like lazy felines.

The day shall dream,

into the corkscrew night.

Last,

would be the stout lantern,

to illuminate our many hands,

as we caress the paper,

with a sturdy pen.

and Yet ...

(there is nothing more attractive than a capital Y)

and Yet ...

this decision is no journey,

and will be made,

only by the guidance.

of our pasty silver moon.

But...

what do we see high,

upon that full face?

Not the resemblance,

of the chalky, cheese filled man.

It is a woman,

who protects her neck.

As the fist presents itself before us,

in defiance of our learned and taught history

that has been

so very, very, lied.

We are the new audience of a natural illumination.

The era soon to be inscribed,

by the multi faced, mad woman moon,

it speaks of all the earth and her past misfortunes,

caused by our sad denials and hysterics.

The Lover Lion Cub

This gentle aggressor,

whose heart could speak no lies,

no wetness glistened,

behind his young, untamed ears.

This shadowy youthed,

thick skinned,

lion cub,

shows times lived,

in eyes far too young.

Eyes, hazeled black, write out the prescriptions,

for those who declare an immunity,

from the natural turns of life.

I have hung limply with no purpose or control,

yet, my heart is a ferocious,

forced gun.

In strength it struggles to persist,

it deciphers the evident future.

My shadow,

chose to lie at the foot,

of a God's altar.

I chose to sit.

in silence,

upon a concrete, dirt filled,

trench.

Comrade shadow?

Gentle death?

I now feel your outline,

fragments of your bony portrait.

Do not deny you own a human face.

If you could turn your strong wooden back,

I could see between your ribs.

Your power is a translucent source.

May I see the other side?

Drawn into an empty space.

This soul cannot be a mere draft echoing,

against some hollow bones.

I am living within this mind's house,

it is the keeper of books.

I have never betrayed my own form.

<u>Religion</u>

These hearts of ours,

have held many traditions,

I can see myself,

within the reflection of your iris.

I find a realization,

that we have lost *their* use,

for we seem to use traditions as ornamentations,

never for their truth of nature.

Residence

There are graveyards on the day of Christ,

that exist, minus prints.

No mark of visitation,

to the home of the dead.

No snow is disturbed,

upon the graves,

assumed to be cold.

I push down the soil,

my effort is to disturb,

the ones,

who are allowed to rest,

upon the best beds,

ever produced.

I took upon myself,

the task,

of walking within the hollowness,

of this place,

to provide the

ponderous prints

of placement.

To mark a visitation.

In this residence,

the stones are too low,

to allow the wind to whistle.

There are trees,

that are here,

that are cold and hard,

and as untouched

as our hearts.

We all claim,

that we have felt them,

being broken.

I feel my heart,

beating under my bone and skin.

My heart and I intend to burn,

indeed I will,

indeed I will,

and be warm!

I wish to be scattered,

where I may no longer be found.

Momentarily ...

I may exist

upon a victims white linens,

upon their well used washing line.

I may be a smudge on a rock weathered dry.

I may spread out as a blanket,

of snow,

encompassing.

I wish to envelop,

not coffin contain.

I have never

found a bed,

worth buying.

Contraction

Verbal lie.

Physical lie.

Lie

left by right,

by left eye,

inter circle,

and outer side.

Deny and forbid,

the devouring dissection,

of the Orifice's intellect.

To appeal,

we will.

To repel,

we wish.

To repeat,

we suffer.

The sand timer,

only owns,

our adolescent

squeals.

Freedom

Isis and Osiris,

divide the splendour of keys.

They no longer entice those,

who's perception and will,

accompany the damnation,

of potential.

To own potential,

provides an intolerance,

by one's peers.

It is gross manipulation,

to stunt one's gifts.

A visualization indeed!

Induced,

by the malignance,

of social inadequacy.

To be taunted,

to be disgraced.

To learn to suffer,

and to survive.

Those,

who have no persistence,

to,

feed their existence,

may only

fall.

Backward wind

We have...

We have not...

We have made love,

we have made

wars.

We have planted no seed,

that has not been harvested before,

the crops have been sown.

Are we not empowered?

Enriched,

seasoned?

By the moments,

of our impotency?

Sunday Drive

The reluctance of acceptance,

is truly defined and condemned,

by those who have had the chance,

to be damned.

In this flag post nation,

where we wear

the blinking,

paper heart,

we are ruined,

by the slightest,

undetermined sound.

We condemn those who appal us,

and swear that our thoughts,

are original creations.

Yellow

d-i-v-i-d-i-n-g

lines.

A religion is only perception,

created by rolling tongues,

and thirsty minds.

Beings deceived

and sensing the deception.

These are the reasons

why my words,

have been placed in this,

trusty pen.

Mansfield 1989

A question I could not answer,

he asked.

I admitted that I had no explanation.

I lacked the courage.

He frowned, unknowingly.

Hunching over his knees,

they came close to his face.

He held his knees,

by holding his fingers.

locked together.

His pinkies hung loosely...

The willow tree,

swept over the crowd of grasses,

as the leaves whistled.

I wept,

as he caressed my forehead.

His legs embraced me,

I was warm.

They smoked,

watching only the glass of the window,

there was no view.

The glass rippled,

it contracted,

expanded,

as the wind,

was marooned.

It wheezed ...

as it coughed up the spoons,

the tea cups fell.

The door squeaked open.

The cups shattered,

as the door raced,

to meet the wall.

The tea lay wet,

and dripping,

ripped,

thrown,

from its bag.

They turned slowly ...

exhaled their smoke.

We acknowledged,

yawned,

both rolled over.

The Beatles did not bother

us.

All four.

We were too asleep,

as we smoked,

wept,

pondered,

and deceived.

We slept, with our eyes open.

Our eyes,

our eyes,

the bottoms of the spiralling teacups,

still intact,

yet brittle, and unappealing.

<u>Anger</u>

Begins,

with hardened, clenched teeth.

Ends, with tongue biting madness.

A pain that dwells,

more than its willingness,

to linger.

A reluctant

repression.

Bruises,

willing to become

wounds.

Words overflowing

in nothingness.

The hectic transfiguration

of time.

Elements.

Human physicalities,

fearful frailties,

Abandoned necessities,

used once,

for survival.

Avoidable questions,

forced to be answered.

Each

turn

into

calico ribbons.

Heart shadow

If there is this unseen moon,

silver, binding,

round, and full.

Why is there

this emptiness left,

within?

Cultivate, cultivate,

farm and sow it.

I have worn out,

every action.

Too many words,

written and rewritten,

just,

in different orders.

The same events,

the same planets.

Digesting,

further digestion,

nothing left to excrete.

My body,

lives

of

itself.

Remembering past episodes,

of my life.

Same charcoal,

once used,

too often.

I heard crickets

in the night.

Were those children...

playing,

in

the

moon

light?

Jessica asks the darkness at 5:00 a.m.

" How old is Victor? "

I answered her in the morning,

when

she remembered

the dream.

" 23 in October, he is Libran."

Stars work too effectively,

at times.

I wear the pentacle tonight,
Blackened from everyday.

The imperfect circle,

too bright to stare at,

causes a crease,

across,

the surprised retina.

This moon was tranquillity,

at Susan's.

Seemed like a liquid silver,

at Susan's.

It covered with no discretion,

at

Susan's.

The old hunter Luna, places her emotions aside,

uses a visual sting.

What may I earn through,

her solitude?

My own defence.

My own securities.

The power of,

intellectual perception?

I should consume.

until I am obese.

What use,

is there for,

paternal protection,

in my life?

what if I still search,

when lying on the Death's bed?

How much time could I remember

investing?

Is this the task,

that has

no

completion?

Is this

the loneliness?

The loneliness

that I have

come

to fear?

Diary of Four Victims

I am one.

My permanent negative solutions.

I will not fall,

as a victim,

in this eternal boredom.

Boredom is a lure,

the denial of excitement.

The foreboding hand,

offers the method,

but not always the means.

It is a doctrine,

of pain,

discomfort is the permanent solution.

Only a shallow hole of happiness,

may be achieved,

and maintained.

It appears as a gift,

it,

is a damnation of life.

Consuming that which is weaker,

to heal one's own weakness.

Homicide is the generation of personal power,

it serves those who need verification,

of their own existence.

They are but jigsaws,

with their pieces scattered,

possibly

even poisoned with an impurity,

caused by their very own

inhuman

nature.

If they do not kill

they leave no mark,

no sub

cycles,

would exist,

after termination.

One hour of suffering.

It was shorter this time,

perhaps he was tired.

I am afraid.

A train, will come before I have crossed the bridge,

before I have travelled to the other side.

It will dismember me,

and spread my limbs across the sleek rails,

embed my corpse within the coal,

and I,

will become fossilized.

The hand of fate forces out its humour,

which lacks the comedy.

And yet...

I cross the tracks slowly.

I am reaching!

Trying to grasp a new thought,

in order to relieve myself,

from impatience.

Life has betrayed me,

the hand of fate has not

supplied my soul,

with a safe passage.

I could grab its thick body,

crushing its form against that wall,

leaving waxy residues,

in the pockets,

of the apron.

Quite gently.

I could take my fingers,

and snuff,

it out.....

leaving me to wait,

wait

with impatience,

within a darkness,

and scream out

the colours of blue-yeller.

My bruises.

My existence causes my disability,

of not being able to create a true silence.

There is little known silence,

in this wound of a world.

It is the taste of soap forced into my mouth.

An order,

to abide and obey the authoritarian.

Forced hard,

down into my throat,

it caused my eyes to water,

it caused my heart to beat,

caused my lungs to swell with impatience

when the next breath did not arrive.

I feel,

I feel,

I feel, that I must still avoid those words.

1. Place an emotional restriction ... it is the best defence.

2. Sustain a high emotional tolerance .... a high physical pain threshold will develop.

3. Pretend that you are an object ... stored and imprisoned within a capsule.

4. Pretend that you are a planet ... held ... yet moving fast throughout the entire universe... for fucks sakes just keep moving ... MOVE !!!

5. Do not move in groups where all have been marked.

6. Do not provide your own movement.

dominoes.

7. Divide your soul.

No words,

no signs,

no visions,

no angels,

no miracles,

have arrived to ensure validation,

of my pursuit.

I grow tired of

falling

to my knees,

on the dirty pew,

for the needs of others ...

sacrificing my spirit,

piece by piece,

for the needs of others.

No prayers are ever answered.

I had never wanted to be part of a social order,

Every dawn, is another man's dirty deeds.

I am number two.

There is no service,

in allowing one's soul to become the chalk stick,

to be placed upon the cinders.

It is always hot,

but never allowed to be burnt.

Beyond recognition.

Beyond reconciliation.

Immortality is a gift of time,

it allows an adequate pursual.

I may kill all of my good actions.

I will never fall victim,

to eternal boredom.

One must burn the tips of their fingers,

before they are fortunate enough,

to be relieved from the darkness.

... and yet,

the flame is but a surrender,

of judgement,

to a mindless man.

A flames energy is stored in contempt,

of being controlled.

Its energy is created,

to be spent and to be fed,

until it destroys.

This is,

its sustenance.

Its gift of,

a very explosive,

consumptive life.

A flame consumes only the wood that is dry

and well preserved.

The flame is a constant symbol of the termination

of another cycle.
The flame is an external tool for creating endurance
for the maintenance of memory.

These flames are heavy,
these flames are thick,

forty-seven burns deep.

They no longer
lick the humidity of the air,
there is no tongue connected,
to the empty palette.

They burn deep,
down.
Leaving the empty tube
hollow.

They burn a mountain,
of molten,
melting fat,
as the wick is consumed too fast,
like the life of me, a fattened man.

I was never asked
to be entrusted.

I had never been asked to be given a gift,

of knowledge,

or a gift with purpose.

My life is a flame,

that could be readily,

extinguished.

These laws

we have all created.

We are all to blame.

I am number three

AM no more,

am no more.

Immortality is a gift of time,

it could allow me a suitable attempt,

to pursue my dreams.

Suicide is a gratification of patience,

the end of a cycle falsely recognized,

as complete.

Survival can feel as if it is won.

It could be seen as a religious facade,

for those who think they lack

useful talents,

within their spirit.

Allow me,

to find wings of a permanent nature.

Allow me,

a longer escape from imprisonment,

within another degenerate,

human,

form.

It only lives to wait

for its eventual death,

or continual dissatisfaction.

Many items ... objects ... organisms ...

have had to die needlessly for object ... X.

Yes, object X, with more vibrancy...

but less endurance.

It may live far past its natural term.

The weak of mind and mass do always return

It is their interlocking fibres

(the strength of),

the true enduring fortitude of

a certain type of soul.

One that generates a certain type of persistence,

it always finds an alternate way,

to be reborn.

Fuel,

to ensure a longer duration.

They hide and hunt,

scatter their souls,

divide it amongst their children.

Until ...

no person is left,

with a soul that is purely their own.

No one,

that I have ever found,

is willing to keep their purity.

They only want to return,

to their natural,

hardened

sedate, existence.

Home is at the end,

of an empty railway tunnel.

I stand at one end of the tunnel,

wanting to go home,

waiting,

to see if there is a safe passage.

I could move freely if I removed my limbs,

pull out my spine.

Like extracting a splinter from the skin.

Remove my structure in order that I could melt.

Slither into some dark catacomb.

I could see the benefits,

of having tooth, nail,

and tongue,

if I lacked the other appendages.

If I terminated,

the incomplete cycles.

Light may be removed,

so that the world,

a voice will disintegrate,

before your eyes.

Hide within the shadows,

by becoming a shadow.

You may prefer to turn your back,

to the window,

in preference for the wall.

force the horrors of life to vanish.

A gunshot fading,

after the crime has been committed.

the silence is sudden,

the silence is temporary.

An exhale.

Your existence has a disability,

it is not allowed,

to create silence.

Smell can be extinguished.

Plug the nostrils,

with two useful fingers,

Name an odour that does not repeat,

or repel a memory.

One that has fallen behind the shelves,

of the mind.

Every dawn is another man's,

dirty deeds.

Who?

Who?

W__?

but a child,

could create,

or at least maintain,

the daydream?

My mind is a bible.

My confessions are silent.

I am Number four,

I was number one,

I was number two,

I was number three,

I place my memories,

within stones,

that carry no other significance,

to any other individual.

They have proven to be useful,

for this purpose.

They hold good information,

my past,

my individual history,

my maintenance.

This is an arduous task, where no adventure is found,

in the search for stones, that have been lost.

Upon the grange field,

upon the beach I walk and collect,

fragments of memory.

Words, phrases,

impermanent images,

and desires.

Wanted lovers

living,

long after their bones,

have been buried.

Their memories are kept,

in the earthen womb.

They execute an existence,

in my memory.

A genetic symbol,

an archetypal photograph

embedded,

within these stones.

Crushed, scattered,
powdered, rounded.
One fragmented piece,

is ample,

to produce a ration of memory.

They are keys used,
to expose my mind,
and my heart.

I have excavated deep
within the earth,
to find,
one solitary blood cell.

After...
soiled and beaten,
I am frequently left with a letter,
a word,
a last name.
They paint pictures,
of a second, a minute,
one brilliant year,

all previously forgotten.

These rocks,
I throw them out.
Back to their nature.
Sedate,
and hard.

It is practice for me,
to discard.

It is custom,
it is a necessity.

I have watched 46 candles burn,
in the form of strangers,
who pass under the street light.
We are all on our way home.

Silence retrieves and revives,
the memory that we have not died.

The faint buzzing of the refrigerator,
electrical light sockets,
the perpetual drip of female faucets,
dishes cleaned,
metallic knots popping.

The tapping of a foot,

a rustle,

a creaking chair,

the squeak of my bed.

I feel, I feel...

that in the end,

I will live my life.

I never wanted to be trusted.

My ten commandments,

have multiplied into sixty,

"Now cafe"

Desperation is a moonbeam,

that provides a highway,

with no divisions of yellow lines.

Conversation is a Sparrow,

that refuses to fly.

Black wings spreading,

the Sparrow wishes to be the Falcon,

to be glorified into,

the predator.

In order to be,

90

more than the prey.

Love is a daydream,

where there are no shadows,

which could reveal a fallacy,

of the highway

that loses its road signs.

Revelation is a cup of coffee,

that gives up,

the stimulus to survive.

Hatred of Silence

Time floats,

like ribbons

falling from hair.

What fear lies within hidden rooms?

Only spider webs, mops and brooms,

and hearts adorning crosses,

for those who have died.

What spirit fades deep inside?

Hello,

sir sorrow,

my close abusive friend,

I call on you to borrow,

verses for these hands.

I have found the restriction,

where are the poems,

left for me write?

To serve as my companions,

within the brassy night?

Ode to Ayn Rand

What of words spoken from floral tongues?

Do we dare pluck the petals to reveal the thorns?

Beauty is a surface well polished,

oiled and difficult to maintain.

Idealism is the craft,

that leads to one's own betrayal.

And yet,

life tends to be richer,

when it is less real.

Reality is a daydream,

abstracted,

it erodes our minds and spirit.

92

A decision,

is a sacrifice of our right to exist.

Language is our crisis,

used to decorate the indecent,

it contradicts all the evidence,

of our statements.

What is derived?

An empty state.

Ashes - ample evidence of a lifetime,

with fingerprints and fabric threads.

What is devised by uncertainty?

Silence of the frustrated screams.

Are we not all exploring?

Blindly for

memorable contact,

with that *substance*,

that merely, might be,

the mythical ... *self*.

A return to alcohol

What face is this, within my bed,

lying within the lover's breath.

He heaves a snore and turns his neck,

away from my pondering eyes.

I feel a heartbeat, a gentle sigh of ill content.

Troubled,

a sign upon the furrowed brow.

So, I kiss his cheek,

so that he ...

may reinvent the dreams,

that thieved him,

of a well earned sleep.

He wakes with a troubled heart,

sitting at the edge,

of this makeshift bed.

Strokes the sheets with fingertips.

He stares

within the murky room,

that cries of buried contempt.

Icy eyes

from the depths of conscious minds,

cannot erase,

the tragedy perceived.

One million baths cannot prevent,

the fuelling marks,

of the new disease.

The deception

My lover spits seeds of lies.

My heart captures this seed to grow,

and poisons the veins of care.

Who could chase my spirit

Only to keep it at bay?

What stain of time,

keeps me waiting

with displeasure?

Oh ...

the torment of scissors,

cut my hair,

cut my hair,

until none is left,

than only skin remains.

Bastards and bitches are circling the home,
that misery is mine, I do not feel the grand sensation.

Cerridwen,
Cerridwen,
Cauldron,
pot,
could I dismember
a penis?

No, it is my heart,
not the worm.

What should I cut first?
Perhaps my hands,

let them be useless.
Perhaps my face,

let it be domesticated.
Perhaps my penis,

I have no service.

Perhaps my heart,

it has believed too much.

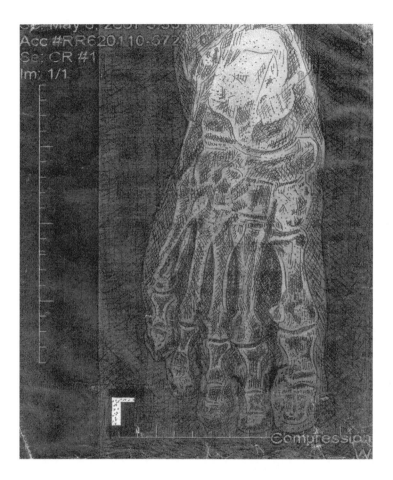

The end of cycle one

I sat,

with the book,

in my lap.

Well spent,

it is.

My beloved friend.

I bid it farewell,

as a constant companion.

No longer another weight,

within the sack.

I let it rest in completion,

with its importance.

It passes the pen,

to my sister hand,

the receiver of numbers,

names and myths.

She is the receiver of my past fortunes,

the letters not received,

words to be spoken,

written and lived.

I smile

with the awkward separation,

as the last spaces are filled.

I leave it here,

with a last embrace against my chest.

Cyclist two, my health

Your spirit had lingered upon our first meeting.

I was chaired, as you skipped through that psychic swing.

My pendulum heart was wielding,

as I caught your scent.

As I channelled into your breathing,

First hand, it was your spirit that I had loved.

Then, I cast the spell of woven lines,

that adopted the spaces around your figure,

across those wide thumbs, and separated eyes.

I played the piano into the evening,

to place that ringing in your ears.

I burnt the herbs and blew them out to you.

How smoke travels even when it cannot be seen,

it fell,

sifted through that first storm,

you desired so much,

to have.

I caressed you and dug into the heart,

yet not deeply,

for there are private things,

those I leave to your secrecy.

I changed the temperature, reduced the heat,

and was not burnt.

Arranged a colour scheme,

placed it over your sleepy eyes and face.

I left a seed, and its provisions,

I had hoped that you would tend it.

Yet now, we seem to have broken.

Perhaps this is the problem with spells,

they are not immune to the flux of seasons

and heart swells.

There are two ships that had drifted side by side,

yet we have sensed the difference of the current.

There is now the decision at hand,

first hand, once again.

Do we paddle, to save from parting?

Do we rise

onto the other's ship?

Do we watch as the sun sets,

and allow two separate ships to drift,

naturally

into their preferred directions?

Damage

Fall into my arms,

and liberate the pain.

You will feel loved,

and I will feel needed.

What damage is there in my embrace?

We lay in the bed,

each bed,

yours and mine.

Each night I have struck you,

within my sleep,

For purposes unknown,

Fall from your fear,

and liberate the coward.

You will feel vulnerable,

and I will be a suspect,

for the damage was done,

long before I arrived.

<u>Three</u>

Past mistakes find their remedies,

in the presence of eventuality.

The present is continuous,

yet, within moments,

it is the past.

Your future is built,

Upon the previous and the current.

Like time, it never stops fleeting,

The world never stops whirling,

The sun never stops soaring and sweeping.

This is the beginning of your life,

 and the ending of the tattered.

In twenty years, you may remark again,

"this is the true creation.

I shall maintain all of the seasons.

My age, it is my history,

and my fountain."

In thirty,

fifty, more,

you shall admit,

" I am old".

Midsummer

Darkness reigns, midsummer eve,

Avvagddu trembles,

his black sombre wings.

Sea storms whisk,

through chestnut trees,

while I sit and smoke,

the autumn leaves.

He reclaims the scent,

as he sails.

Charms the dead,

from measured entrails.

He burnt my back,

as I carved the thicket.

Blistered my thumbs,

between their cracks.

He saved the bubbles as souvenirs,

cackled at my pain,

and split my tears.

I am solitary once again.

Farthest from fireside,

I find the harness,

 of my old friend.

The paintings are unfinished,

yet they stare,

they are plenty perfect,

they hold their own lives.

The wind is scourging,

with its rainy knives.

The gale is calling,

for my spirit to heal.

It bids for the mending,

within the winds.

Avvagddu is proclaiming,

 the Underworld swims.

<u>Crown</u>

Now, my heart is opened up,

yet where is the lover,

who will direct the pain?

There is no waiting spouse,

to deceive my deliverance,

(nor even a slight caress).

Who now, shall provide a shadow?

As I cut my fingers open,

they have become blistered.

I try to obsess, about the work.

My dove spirit has broken its wing,

it hides in the shadows

of some scarred rooftop device.

It fears its own mortality.

It imagines the possibilities,

the end with no proper burial,

starving

as the resources

deplete.

It searches for its escape,

it's possibilities...

To plummet to the ground,

in an awkward fluttered frenzy?

It would give the spirit a chance,

to run.

Or at least avoid

hitting the pavement.

<u>Carving</u>

I am bleeding myself into recovery.

The spots and stars are growing thin,

in the melting of my icy veins.

Blue,

it seemed,

between my squinting eyes.

Yet, red it flowed,

when I went to catch the drop.

In, it curved,

around my arm,

to leave its stain.

It resists leaving the warmth of my heart.

It too,

can feel the pulse,

even so far past

the knifey elbow.

I bled,

and pouted softly.

Looking over,

the purple painted door,

the sun winced in disgust.

Ruffling its cloudy cloak,

it went out,

to be entertained elsewhere.

Drip ... drip ... drip ...
It dives to the floor,
and sinks in.

Flat lying,
my exiled spot looks up from the reason,
its face imitates my own.
It does not know,
where to walk.

Lies ...
Sticking slowly.
Life being sucked dry,
by the bones of wood.

Its eyes slowly shutting.
Nodding off to death,
it looks to its brothers,
who are winding,
suspending about my arm.

Aboriginal

Large.

She is a healing woman,

draped in purple blouses.

Her wide, brown face gleams,

with her saturation,

of information.

She leaves footprints, always,

when she walks.

Fingerprints are on every surface,

and her scent

lingers.

Her voice shivers through the walls,

out the windows.

I can hear her two floors away.

The birds have begun to chirp.

Sam pours milk into plastic cups.

... 2 ... cups.

She still smiles,

waits, sways softly.

Beside her,

they too,

pick up her rhythms,

not revealing that, but they waiver.

She is laughing,

as Sam,

is busily confused.

She is hungry.

Her hands hold

her keys,

they began to jingle.

She ... is still,

and smiling.

The Sister's Hand

I had a lover who refused to die,

within these limbs.

I passed the work onto my sister,

who waited outside the door.

The door did not open to strangers.

I owned familiarity,

within the bed,

coffin craft,

altar shaft.

I had a cocoon made of unravelled thread,

colours caught upon nails loosened,

through life, and breath.

I have found myself the stranger,

amongst an island of men.

All have felt my "permanent" caress.

I drew on all their bloods.

I cried out,

in an empty silence,

to the angel trapped within the ceiling.

Its wings are beaten,

frayed and grey.

It sits, hanging from dead electrical tape.

I constructed an abstract cross,

made it round.

I had a lover,

who's locks of hair remain,

sewn into hair brushes.

Trunks full of toothbrushes,

labelled,

naked

and dry.

Listless nights,

that add up to ...

an end,

while She ...

closes the door to strangers.

<u>Texture</u>

The leer,

is used to defend,

the illiterate self.

My smile,

has one million and three,

entirely different meanings.

My expressions,

are only a change,

in the texture of my skin.

I communicate with my voice,

the medium is the challenge.

Emotion is an achievement,

of texture well consumed.

Farmers Reaping

There is great clarity,

in visions,

so designed,

to improve the pendulums,

created,

by time.

I do not see

death's,

most gallant scythe.

I see the glow of angels,

within

the knives.

They take the form,

of soured seeds,

scattering hearts,

within

the weeds.

They clean the nests,

of the crackled eggs,

fertilize

the herbs,

on

the dead man's grave.

Evolution

I have had many a friend,

yet,

they have all drifted,

into infinity.

They

have become insane,

with the sorrow,

of knowing.

I see them,

often,

recognizing me,

but not by name.

Do they know?

That

I am shining,

from work,

that has ached my muscles?

I am

glowing,

from the fatigue.

I am heightened,

through completion,

of the strenuous task,

that burns my hands.

I am heightened,

by knowing,

the letters which form,

my name.

They produce mantras,

when stated with love.

I say them often,

for I know,

that a time has passed.

I am

no longer capable,

of deceiving,

myself.

I see a friend,

I would call out,

to him.

But,

I

am not

lonely.

114

I had grown tired,

I,

had grown

to be scared,

by living

alone.

Then,

I became ...

comfortable,

with being alone.

Then,

I became happy,

with being alone.

It,

has lost,

its sorrow,

from mourning,

for other voices.

It,

does not hold,

my heart,

with its

fanged mouth.

It
kisses my temples,
my cheeks,
my lips.

It
blesses me,
with independence.

St. Lawrence

If I were to fly a seagull,
over a spotted field,
the waves of grasses blowing,
could tend to your blistered heart.

I could launch,
a widow's web,
out into the brine.
There you may
leap into,
the catacombs of time.

All is not lost,
for those who live in fear.

The callous wind is angry,

it penetrates my ears.

My heart is melting,

my head is draining,

out...

the black depression.

My sister's wings,

sweep across the sky,

while her tail cuts the waves.

I am a burden upon this rock,

I am a cherished weight.

I must find a forest,

that will relieve me.

I am now the jagged stone.

In ten days,

I will be worn,

smooth, and soft,

by my brother's wind.

I will return humble,

and willing,

to dawn again.

A poverty

Close your eyes!

Close your eyes,

there is nothing left to see.

We are the experts that starve,

while it is you,

who will chew on our words,

to soothe your souls.

Close your eyes.

There is a vision,

of my ribs protruding,

from the slightly stretched skin.

This performance,

is not pornographic,

is not a sports event.

It is our riot,

it is our murder.

It is not between the clean comfortable sheets,

where we stretch our feet,

and die.

It is an expression of our pains,

where we,

break our backs.

118

While you,

view it,

and

are entertained.

Do you understand,

that we have not eaten,

a meal of any grade,

today?

We,

will feast on the crumbs,

that you miss on your plates,

after the reception is over.

You,

will walk away fat and affected,

We are starving,

while you sit,

in the comfortable seats.

Rebecca's stone

I love you dear sister,

soul mate of mine.

What bond has chased our hearts into ink?

Upon the landscapes,

of cascading bones,

lay the ruins of our ideal surrender.

And yet,

we combat,

for we share a common womb,

made from different mothers.

We have always been

one and the same.

The words on paper,

identical,

only the hands differ.

Our gender makes you beautiful,

and fertile.

Our gender makes me

different,

black and stinging.

I have been the strings on your violin,

while you have been the sword,

that cuts my fingertips.

How I have wished to seduce you,

recover you as mine,

even though your loins,

those inner chambers,

would turn to silt and stone.

My differing desires,

cause lust to die.

What partnership

does this reflect?

Is it not parallel to the ones,

that we have previously

and readily

survived.

Samhain Spell

Across the skies,

my cooled breath,

swallows the stars,

to give you light.

The cold does not touch,

my silver brow,

as my nakedness

swims through,

your coloured snows.

I breathe into your heart.

So there love flows,

when ice does melt,

upon this,

this vesselled spell.

Within your eager spring,

in your mirror,

I do reside,

blessing you through,

the brassy nights.

I am as near,

as you believe.

Call out my name,

and I shall recall,

this loving spell,

on the Samhain eve.

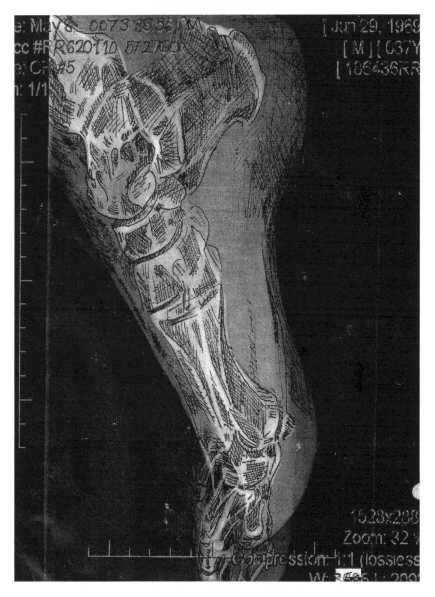

Besom

They are sweeping,

away,

all decay,

left by broken hearted survivors.

They are sweeping,

down,

every sound,

left ...

by the choking cries,

of the disbelievers.

They are sweeping,

waves,

into the days,

left ...

by the stagnant tongues,

of broken bards.

They are sweeping,

hell,

with banging bells,

to awaken the living.

They are sweeping,

all the weeping,

scratching their skins,

so that they may feel.

They are sweeping,

with,

Witch's switches,

flogging the senses,

of the undeserved.

They are sweeping women's wombs,

scratched and scarred,

by the foreign machines.

They are angels,

sweeping with tattered wings.

They are angels,

that resemble,

chimney sweeps.

<u>Whistle</u>

City with no walls,

nor no horns,

no rooms,

nor no doors,

to hold the hearts within the stars.

How long they have cried with the mouths unseen,
Their endowment of the psychic scream.

How long will the wind share their fate,
Upon glass hillsides and across the grates.
How long with no hands, no feet, no tongue,
will the silence continue on?

How many colours are the skins,
that have never felt teeth,
within mouthless grins.
How many shapes of heads are flat,
How many children have felt the slaps.

Songs unsung of molested boys,
songs of girls as their toys.
Ringing distant are the bells,
that steal the children's beloved pelts.

How many skies have burdened their dust,
how many lovers have earned mistrust.

How many scars have I felt,
how many more may I cut out.

Libation

Beauty, beauty,

reflecting glass,

frosted window panes,

crackling silent masts.

Fire!

Fire!

Burn it!

I feel cold.

My heart is frosted,

by a cursed lover's need.

Scars could sew

thistles across,

the sinister skies.

Winter blasts,

summon,

the spider's eggs,

from their confident cobbed web.

It is the warmth of the lover's kiss,

that breaks,

a fisherman's net.

Tremble, needle, scissors, and blood,

they cut through all black specks.

Sand, silt, seed, and snow,

Gifts of winter's kiss.

Heather, cedar, oak moss, orris root.

Sage.

Dragon's blood.

Anise.

Baptist flute.

Damiana teas,

needles through flames,

burning effigies,

and unspoken names.

Flowered skies,

powdered bones,

these are what spells are made of.

Love and thought,

thought in love,

this is what life is made from.

Life in life,

death in death,

this is where I come from.

Groves of trees,

the twelve,

and one.

Dust and stone,

this is where,

all good things grow

Position

Yes...

dear sister,

it is your scent that I love.

Like the blossoming Morning glory,

hallucinogenic, and explosive,

both, I admire.

Then,

as the light wears thin,

you are like the most aged earth,

fertile and enticing.

Your breath owns the cooled tongue,

kisses away,

cooling,

that fiery danger.

How delicate we both were,

with our barb wire defence systems.

Now,

we are raw,

less ornamented,

like old wooden shacks,

and autumn trees.

Our lovemaking,

is running sap,

and yet,

we are always

the siblings,

suffered,

from different wombs.

Hearts are always stranded,

together,

and we still cackle,

titter, teeter,

and giggle.

Many years later,

we still admire the fanciful pictures,

depicting

Kama Sutra.

Micca Wuulwicce retired from being a professional modern dancer in the late 1990's due to multiple foot and back injuries. New beginnings.

Made in the USA
Lexington, KY
08 December 2019